CONTENTS

my little Pony

Pedigree®

Licensed by:
Hasbro

Published by Pedigree Books Limited
Beech Hill House, Walnut Gardens,
Exeter, Devon EX4 4DH
Email: books@pedigreegroup.co.uk
Published 2007
My Little Pony © 2007 Hasbro.
All rights reserved

£6.99

Meet the Ponyville Ponies

Wysteria

Wysteria is one of the sweetest, quietest ponies within Ponyville. Despite being very quiet, Wysteria loves to fill each day with fun and laughter, and generally likes to look upon each day in a positive way. This positivity tends to rub off on her friends, making her a very popular pony indeed.

Minty

Minty is one Pony that you couldn't possibly call boring. From trying to reach the North Pole in a hot air balloon to collecting socks, Minty is certainly one of a kind. With her love of telling jokes and her knack of coming up with crazy ideas, whenever Minty is around there is sure to be some excitement.

Scootaloo

Scootaloo loves butterflies. So much so in fact, that she will often be seen riding around Ponyville on her scooter, looking for even more beautiful specimens to add to her collection. Scootaloo is so proud of this collection that she will often invite her friends over to her house to see it.

Pinkie Pie

Pinkie Pie — like Wysteria - is one of the sweetest of the Ponyville Ponies - although she can also be rather nervous. For example, one time, whilst camping with Sparkleworks, the fireworks above them were so bright and loud that they made her run home in fright - with the tent still on top of her as she ran! What a sight that must have been!

Tink-a-Tink-a-Too

Tink-a-Tink-a-Too is the creative, inventive pony of Ponyville. Her enthusiasm for building and decorating things is well known among her friends and whenever they need to see her, they will often find her working on a hot air balloon, or dashing around Ponyville looking for something she needs for a new invention.

Rainbow Dash

Rainbow Dash is always ready for adventure and can often be found looking for new rainbows that she can ride in Ponyville. When she isn't riding rainbows she will generally be looking for other ways of having fun with her friends. As well as being fun loving, Rainbow Dash is also caring and considerate and loves to look after her friends (or `darlings' as she likes to call them).

Sky Wishes

Sky Wishes will often be found staring up at the night sky, making wishes for every star she sees. These wishes are usually for her friends, although she does have one wish of her own — that she will one day become the greatest dancer in the whole of Ponyville. She knows that this will take a lot of practice, but she also knows that dreams really do come true when you aim for the stars.

Bumbleberry

Bumbleberry loves to makes sweet deserts and will often be joined by her friends wanting to sample her famous Bumbleberry pie — a `sweet-vention' she created using all the best berries of Ponyville's surrounding bushes. Bumbleberry certainly has a sweet tooth, although you'll never catch any of her friends complaining about this.

The Christmas Carol

It was Christmas time in Ponyville and all of the ponies were getting really excited about the upcoming festivities. In the centre of Ponyville at the Ponyville Theatre all the ponies had gathered to see their friends in the Christmas play. It had been a very busy time for the ponies who were involved with the show. They had had to make costumes and sets, and learn all their lines for the play. Everything was nearly ready now though, and the show was about to begin.

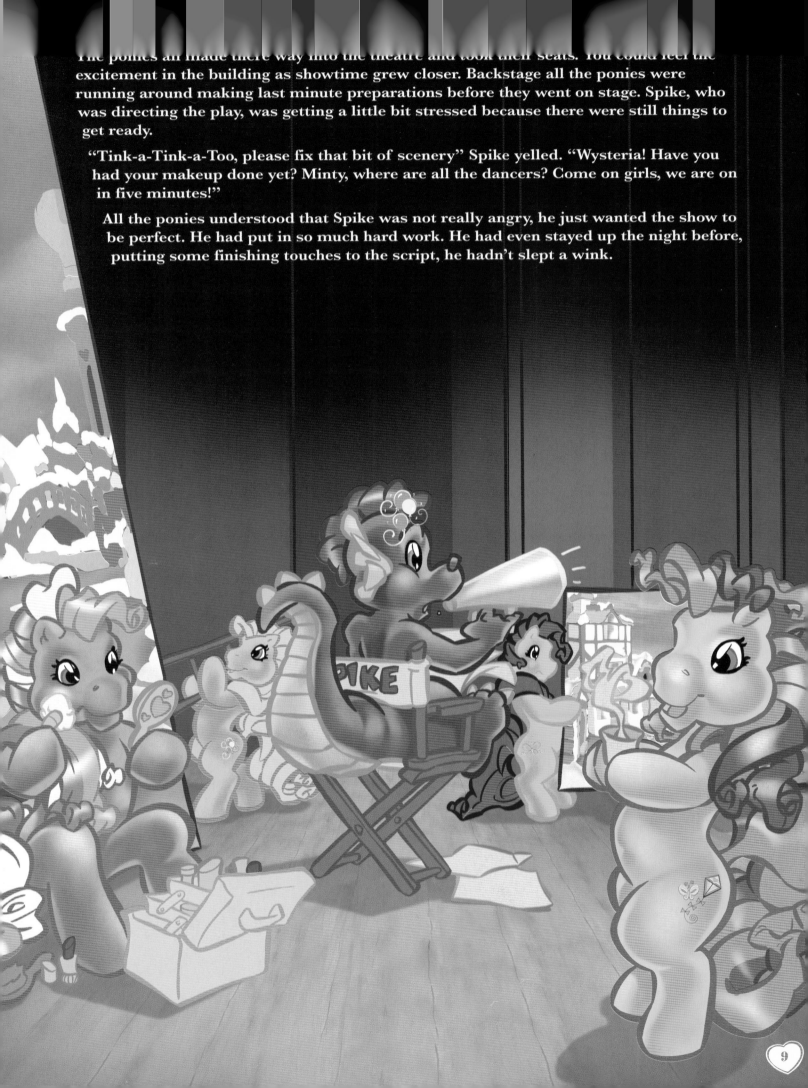

The ponies all made there way into the theatre and took their seats. You could feel the excitement in the building as showtime grew closer. Backstage all the ponies were running around making last minute preparations before they went on stage. Spike, who was directing the play, was getting a little bit stressed because there were still things to get ready.

"Tink-a-Tink-a-Too, please fix that bit of scenery" Spike yelled. "Wysteria! Have you had your makeup done yet? Minty, where are all the dancers? Come on girls, we are on in five minutes!"

All the ponies understood that Spike was not really angry, he just wanted the show to be perfect. He had put in so much hard work. He had even stayed up the night before, putting some finishing touches to the script, he hadn't slept a wink.

Before long, everything was ready and Spike made his way out to the theatre and took his seat. He was so tired. As the curtain opened and the crowd began to cheer, Spike could hardly keep his eyes open. Royal Bouquet walked out onto the stage to introduce the play.

"A long time ago, there was a man who was very mean. He lived on his own in a big old house where he loved to sit and count his money."
Suddenly Spike woke up with a start!
"Oh I must have fallen asleep!" he said to himself.
"Wait a minute, where am I?"
Spike found himself stood in front of a big wooden door. On the door was a large metal knocker in the shape of a ponies face. As he looked at the knocker he thought he recognised the face and then all of the sudden the face moved!
Spike shook his head, rubbed his eyes and looked again.
"Hello" said the knocker!
"Aaah!" Spike yelled as he jumped backward.
"Who are you?"

"Don't you recognise me?" asked the knocker, "I'm your old friend, Wysteria!"

"Wysteria!" exclaimed Spike. "What are you doing in the door knocker?"

"I am here to tell you something, something very important" answered Wysteria, "Come on in and I will tell you all about it!"

Spike opened the door and went inside. He soon realised that he was in his house and in his bedroom.

"Oh" he said to himself, "perhaps I was just dreaming, maybe it was something I ate, a bad piece of cheese. Yes. Cheese. That can make you have funny dreams!"

Spike sat down on his bed. Suddenly something tapped him on the shoulder. Spike jumped up and spun around. "Arrggh!" he cried. It was Wysteria. She was sat behind him on his bed.

"Don't be afraid Spike, there is nothing to be scared of" said Wysteria in a soothing voice.

"Well I wish you would stop making me jump!" said Spike angrily.

"I'm sorry Spike" Wysteria continued, "Would you like to know why I am here?"

"Well I was starting to wonder!" said Spike, still angry that Wysteria had made him jump.

"Tonight you will be visited by three ponies" said Wysteria, "they want to teach you about the true meaning of Christmas."

"I don't have time for that" Spike said abruptly, "I have to get ready for the show."

"Well Spike, the three ponies will be coming anyway. It's very important that you listen to what they have to say."

"I don't want to listen!" said Spike, "I am very tired and I must get some sleep before the show tomorrow. I don't want any visitors tonight no matter how important you say they are!" Spike was getting quite angry now.

"Why won't you just leave me alone? You know how busy I am, and you know I don't like this time of year. I have never enjoyed Christmas. All the presents and all the parties. It's just too busy. I never even liked it when I was a little Dragon. Wysteria, are you listening to me?" Spike ranted. But when Spike turned around, Wysteria was gone. He was alone in his room. Spike put on his pyjamas and night-cap and got into bed.

"Well that told her!" he said to himself. "I won't be getting anymore visitors tonight!"

Spike had been asleep for just a few short hours when he was suddenly woken by a noise. He sat up and looked around his room. He couldn't see anything so he lay back down and closed his eyes.

"Spike" something whispered. Spike jumped out of bed and turned on his light.

"Who's there?" Spike asked. But no one answered. "Oh Spike," he said to himself, "You must be dreaming!" He lay back down on his bed and was about to drop off to sleep again when he heard, "Spike, Spike wake up!" Again Spike jumped out of bed and looked around.

He still couldn't see anybody. He ran over to his cupboard and looked inside. Nothing. He ran back to his bed and looked underneath, still nothing.

"Spike, up here" said the voice again. Spike looked up and floating over his bed was Star Catcher.

"Star Catcher!" Spike exclaimed. "What are you doing here?"

"I am the first of your visits" Star Catcher answered.

"I thought I made it quite clear that I did not want to see anybody tonight!" Spike said grumpily.

"Well I am sorry Spike, but this is very important. Are you ready to go?" asked Star Catcher.

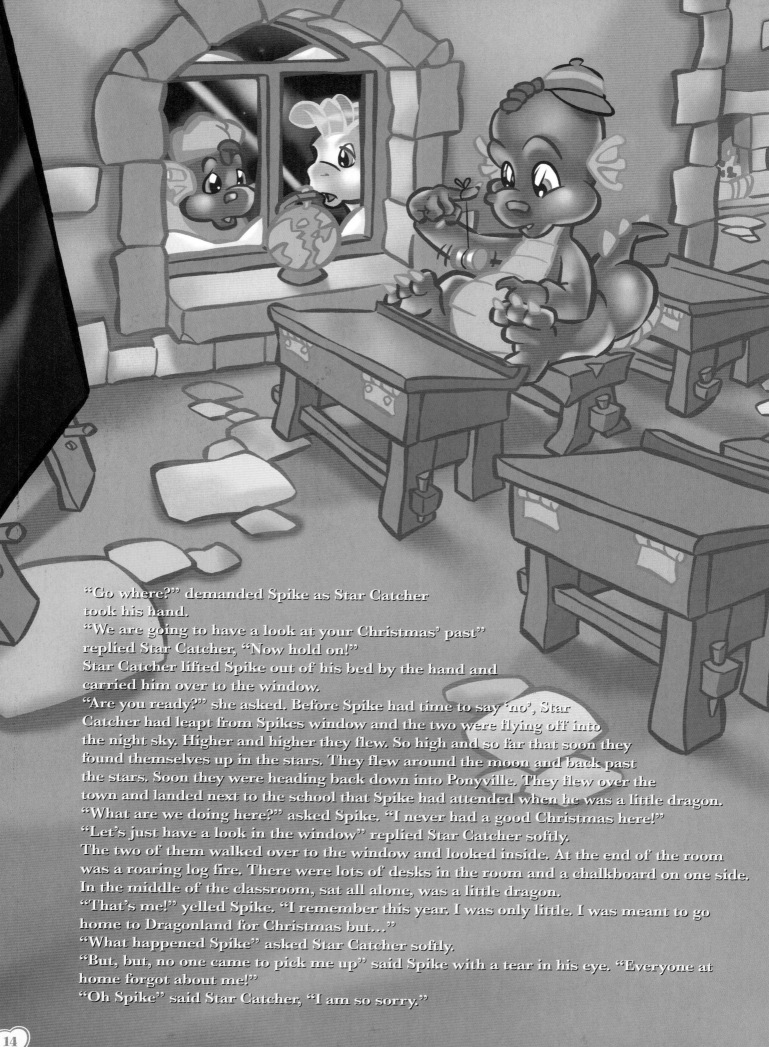

"Go where?" demanded Spike as Star Catcher
took his hand.
"We are going to have a look at your Christmas' past"
replied Star Catcher, "Now hold on!"
Star Catcher lifted Spike out of his bed by the hand and
carried him over to the window.
"Are you ready?" she asked. Before Spike had time to say 'no', Star
Catcher had leapt from Spikes window and the two were flying off into
the night sky. Higher and higher they flew. So high and so far that soon they
found themselves up in the stars. They flew around the moon and back past
the stars. Soon they were heading back down into Ponyville. They flew over the
town and landed next to the school that Spike had attended when he was a little dragon.
"What are we doing here?" asked Spike. "I never had a good Christmas here!"
"Let's just have a look in the window" replied Star Catcher softly.
The two of them walked over to the window and looked inside. At the end of the room
was a roaring log fire. There were lots of desks in the room and a chalkboard on one side.
In the middle of the classroom, sat all alone, was a little dragon.
"That's me!" yelled Spike. "I remember this year. I was only little. I was meant to go
home to Dragonland for Christmas but…"
"What happened Spike" asked Star Catcher softly.
"But, but, no one came to pick me up" said Spike with a tear in his eye. "Everyone at
home forgot about me!"
"Oh Spike" said Star Catcher, "I am so sorry."

"It doesn't matter Star Catcher" said Spike, "I'm sure it was an accident, everyone apologised to me when they remembered me."

"Still though" said Star Catcher, "it is very sad. Do you think that is why you don't like Christmas?"

"No!" said Spike firmly. "That has nothing to do with it! I just don't like Christmas!"

"Please don't get upset Spike" said Star Catcher in a soothing voice, "Shall we move on?"

"Yes please" said Spike wiping his eyes.

Star Catcher took him by the hand and again they flew up into the stars and then back down into Ponyville. This time they landed near Bumbleberry's bakery. They looked into the window and saw lots of ponies having a party. They were eating cake and drinking fizzy fruit punch. They were all having a good time!

"I remember this!" said Spike. You were all having a party and no one invited me!"

"Spike, we all thought you had gone home to see your family. No one knew that you were in Ponyville when we organised the party. Why did you not say anything before?" asked Star Catcher.

"I didn't want to make a fuss" said Spike, still looking through the window, with two little columns of steam coming from his nostrils.

"Is this why you don't like Christmas?" Star Catcher asked again.

"No Star Catcher! I just don't like Christmas" replied Spike with tears again welling up in his eyes.

15

Christmas Cake Recipe

Bumbleberry's quick and simple Christmas cake recipe.

Remember... always ask an adult for help when using sharp tools and cooking equipment.

What you will need to make your cake:

- 8 oz of Flour
- 1 teaspoon of baking powder
- 2 well-beaten eggs
- 1 cup of cold water
- 7oz of sugar
- 1 teaspoon of bicarbonate of soda (baking soda)
- 1 lb of mixed dried fruit
- 4oz of butter
- 1 teaspoon of mixed spice
- Nuts and/or cherries (optional)

What you will need to do:

1: Firstly you will need to sift together the flour and baking powder

2: Secondly you will need to place all other ingredients (EXCEPT FOR THE EGGS) into a saucepan and bring slowly to the boil. (Remember to ask an adult for help with this).

3: You will then need to take this away from the heat.

4: You may then add the sifted flour and baking powder into the mix. The beaten eggs can then be added, although you must ensure you add them last.

5: The mixture should then be poured into a lined cake tin (approx. 8 inches by 5 inches) and baked in the oven for 1 - 1 $\frac{1}{2}$ hours, on the centre shelf, at 180 °C (350 °F: gas mark 5).

Once the cake has cooked, be very careful not to burn yourself on the hot tin. Be sure to let the tin cool down before handling it, as you will then be able to share the cake with your friends and family without burning your fingers.

If you would like to, you can also decorate the cake in order to make it look pretty. You can do this by using red, green, and white icing; the colours we think of when thinking of Christmas.

Christmas word search

Can you help Sunny Daze to find the words hidden within this word search square? The words you are looking for can read backwards, forwards, across, up, down and diagonally. Good luck.

V	F	V	A	R	B	W	O	M	P	G	N	P	V	G	W	K	X	T	C
C	S	Z	K	Z	T	C	H	M	V	T	I	N	S	E	L	M	K	R	U
H	H	T	R	C	N	P	L	L	R	K	P	U	Y	V	Z	P	T	E	E
J	H	H	O	S	Q	M	P	R	E	S	E	N	T	S	I	R	Z	E	I
D	X	U	U	C	G	U	Z	K	D	C	F	W	X	V	S	T	D	L	M
D	J	Z	E	I	K	H	B	N	Z	V	J	Y	S	I	D	Q	R	G	L
V	B	R	F	M	D	I	O	V	W	G	L	U	F	Y	B	Q	C	U	C
B	S	L	V	G	X	E	N	L	N	M	I	S	T	L	E	T	O	E	E
K	K	S	C	C	Y	M	A	G	L	F	J	H	A	Y	S	T	A	R	C
T	O	V	L	W	J	M	U	C	C	Y	G	D	Y	I	J	O	I	F	S
C	Y	P	C	H	R	I	S	T	M	A	S	T	Y	O	N	R	V	Q	A
M	R	Q	C	T	F	Q	C	F	W	I	I	K	E	N	Z	G	R	S	N
I	Z	V	T	O	S	X	H	Q	L	R	Q	V	L	H	G	Z	O	S	T
N	V	M	I	P	E	L	V	E	S	T	A	N	F	N	M	P	Q	A	A
C	U	X	T	F	F	M	O	V	G	S	N	O	W	W	J	T	U	C	M
E	R	E	E	I	W	E	Z	L	Y	Q	S	S	M	R	D	M	M	R	D
P	W	X	V	O	O	O	E	Y	H	W	S	W	P	Z	G	O	D	A	R
I	T	C	M	W	E	V	A	K	R	F	O	Y	A	I	D	V	V	E	P
E	C	A	R	O	L	S	B	Y	Y	V	L	L	R	T	E	I	K	M	N
S	G	W	H	E	C	T	R	A	M	M	K	Q	O	L	M	O	F	C	K

- [ ] **CHRISTMAS**
- [ ] **SANTA**
- [ ] **CAROLS**
- [ ] **PRESENTS**
- [ ] **TREE**
- [ ] **STAR**
- [ ] **MISTLETOE**
- [ ] **STOCKING**
- [ ] **TINSEL**
- [ ] **SNOW**
- [ ] **MINCEPIES**
- [ ] **ELVES**
- [ ] **HOLLY**

Can you solve the Pony Christmas Cross Word?

Look at the clues and try to work out the answers. Good luck!

Across

1. A Pony's favourite way to travel
2. He brings you presents at Christmas time
3. Where do all the ponies live?
4. A Pony that just loves pancakes

Down

5. At Christmas you might bake one of these.

6. The only pony to have ridden every rainbow in Ponyville.
7. In winter, this falls from the sky.
8. On Christmas Day, if you've been good, you'll get some of these.
9. When you wrap up presents you might tie one of these around them.
10. You keep all off you presents under this.

Star Catcher and Spike left Bumbleberry's bakery and flew back through the stars to Spikes bedroom. They landed softly on the bed and Spike started to cry.

"Oh Spike, don't be sad, "said Star Catcher "It will soon be Christmas again and this year will be the best Christmas you have ever had."

"No it won't" cried Spike, "I have never had a good Christmas before so why should this one be any different!"

"Well you will soon see" said Star Catcher.

"I don't want to see. I'm going to stay in bed all Christmas and not even go out. Now leave me alone!" said Spike, pulling his bedclothes over his head.

"Okay Spike" said Star Catcher in her most comforting voice, "I am going to go now but remember, you will have another two visits tonight."

Star Catcher stepped back onto the window ledge and flew away into the night.

Spike ran to the window and pulled it shut. He made sure to lock it.

"I don't want to have anymore visits tonight!" Spike sniffed as he wrapped himself up in his blanket and went to sleep.

Spike had been asleep for a short while before he heard a 'rat-a-tat-tat' on his window. Spike rolled himself up even tighter in his bedclothes and buried his head under the pillow. 'Rat-a-tat-tat' went the window again. Spike pretended he was asleep, making snoring noises, but the tapping at the window carried on. Eventually Spike couldn't take it any more and ran over to the window and flung it open.

"Who's there?" he shouted, "What do you want? I'm trying to sleep!"

"I'm your second visit" a voice behind him said.

"What?!" Spike spun around to see Pinkie Pie bouncing on his bed.

"How…how…how did you get in?" Spike asked confused.

"You left your door open" replied Pinkie Pie with a giggle.

"Mmmmmm!" grumbled Spike. "Well what is it you want at this time of night?"

"I am going to show you your Christmas Present" replied Pinkie Pie.

"My Christmas present!" exclaimed Spike, "I've never had a Christmas present before!"

"No Spike" chuckled Pinkie Pie, "Not that kind of present, present like past and present!"

"Oh" Spike said dejectedly, "Well I don't want to see that! I'm going back to bed!"

"No, no no," Pinkie Pie said firmly, "You need to come with me if you want to make your Christmas' better!" Pinkie Pie grabbed Spike and ran out into the street.

As they stepped outside the street began to change from night to day. Ponies appeared in the street rushing around, carrying presents and chatting happily to each other.

"What's going on?" asked Spike.

"It's Christmas Day" said Pinkie Pie, "everyone is giving each other presents and getting ready for Christmas dinner!"

"Well I don't like it!" said Spike firmly, "I want to go home!"

"Wait a minute Spike" said Pinkie Pie, "let's go see what people are up to!"

Pinkie Pie grabbed Spikes hand and led him over to Twinkle Twirls dance studio. They opened the door and went inside.

"I don't think they can see us" said Spike.

"No, they can't. Remember we are in the future and this is magic. We're invisible!" explained Pinkie Pie.

They walked into Twinkle Twirls dance room where some of the ponies were having a party. It looked like great fun. The ponies were dancing and singing and exchanging presents witheach other. Scootaloo was there with Minty. Spike and Pinkie Pie listened to what they were saying…

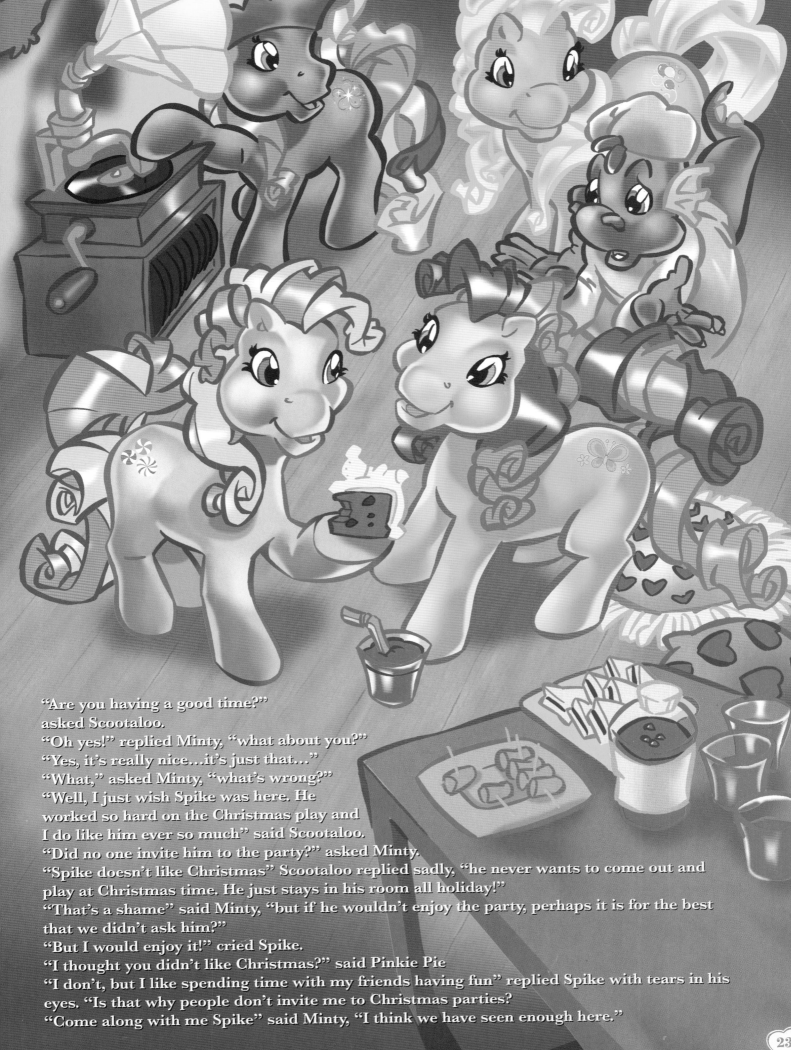

"Are you having a good time?"
asked Scootaloo.
"Oh yes!" replied Minty, "what about you?"
"Yes, it's really nice…it's just that…"
"What," asked Minty, "what's wrong?"
"Well, I just wish Spike was here. He
worked so hard on the Christmas play and
I do like him ever so much" said Scootaloo.
"Did no one invite him to the party?" asked Minty.
"Spike doesn't like Christmas" Scootaloo replied sadly, "he never wants to come out and
play at Christmas time. He just stays in his room all holiday!"
"That's a shame" said Minty, "but if he wouldn't enjoy the party, perhaps it is for the best
that we didn't ask him?"
"But I would enjoy it!" cried Spike.
"I thought you didn't like Christmas?" said Pinkie Pie
"I don't, but I like spending time with my friends having fun" replied Spike with tears in his
eyes. "Is that why people don't invite me to Christmas parties?
"Come along with me Spike" said Minty, "I think we have seen enough here."

Pinkie Pie led Spike over to the other side of Ponyville and to a house he hadn't seen before. "Who lives here?" Spike asked.

"No one knows her name" replied Pinkie Pie.

The two of them peered into the tiny, run down house. What they saw would bring a tear to the eye of even the sternest person. A pony was sat all alone at a table with just a candle to keep her warm. There were no decorations in the house, no sign of any presents, in fact no sign of Christmas at all.

"Why does she look so sad?" asked Spike.

"Maybe it's because she doesn't have anyone to share Christmas with," replied Pinkie Pie, "you're not the only one in Ponyville that finds Christmas hard."

"Really?" asked Spike.

"Some people don't have any friends or family to share the holiday with," Pinkie Pie explained, "and some people don't have the money to buy expensive presents or to decorate their house."

"I wish I could do something to make her happy" said Spike.

"Maybe someday you will be able to" said Pinkie Pie with a smile.

"Pinkie Pie" said Spike, "I don't know why you and Star Catcher have come to visit me tonight, but I am glad that you did."

"Are you starting to change your mind about Christmas?" asked Pinkie Pie.

"Maybe," replied Spike, "I can see how it could be fun to spend time with my friends, and maybe even swap presents with each other. But when I look at this poor little pony, sat alone, it makes me sad."

"It makes me sad too Spike" said Pinkie Pie, "It's nearly time for me to go, shall we go back to your house now?

"Yes please" said Spike looking at Pinkie Pie, "I wish you could stay a little longer."

"Oh don't worry Spike, you'll soon see me again" said Pinkie Pie.

The two of them walked back to Spike's house through Ponyville where everyone was still dashing around, carrying their presents and wishing each other a very merry Christmas. Some of the ponies were standing around a fire and roasting chestnuts and marshmallows. Others were singing carols while there friends listened and clapped along.

The whole of Ponyville was blanketed in a thick layer of fluffy white snow. Ponies were building snowmen, and having snowball fights. Some of them were even sledging and skiing down the hill. Everyone was having such a lovely time. Spike and Pinkie Pie arrived back at his house. "I don't want to go back to bed" said Spike, "it's so much fun out here!"

"You have to," said Pinkie Pie, "Remember you still have one more visit due to you tonight."
"Who will it be?" asked Spike.
"Your final visitor tonight will be the Pony of Christmas Yet To Come" replied Pinkie Pie.
"What does that mean?" asked Spike.
"This pony will show you what will happen in the future" said Pinkie Pie.
"I'm not sure I want to see that" said Spike looking a little nervous.
"Remember Spike" said Pinkie Pie, "your future is not set in stone, you still have time to change it."
"How?" asked Spike, but before he could get an answer the street started to fade away and he found himself lying in his bed, once again.

Spot the difference!

Look at the two pictures of Minty's house at Christmas, and see if you can spot the five differences between them. Good luck.

1. Tree decorations, 2. Christmas Garland, 3. Fireplace stocking, 4. Christmas present sack, 5. Plate of cookies.

29

My Little Pony Christmas Poem

With Christmas day approaching,
excitement was growing fast,
and all the ponies of Ponyville,
were glad it had come at last.

Presents were wrapped and ready,
and tinsel was on the tree.
The ground was covered with pure white snow
all ponies were filled with glee.

Minty was the first to yell,
"Merry Christmas everyone."
Then Cupcake giggled and said to her,
"Thanks Minty - let's have some fun."

First they wrapped up nice and warm,
before rushing from the house.
Scooping up the cold snow in their hands,
they began to throw it about.

Sweetberry threw a snowball,
that hit sweet breeze on the nose,
Then all the other ponies joined in,
until all had frozen toes.

"Let's get back into the house,"
said Sky Wishes with a sneeze.
"I think my tail's about to fall off,
or at least it's going to freeze."

"Good idea," answered Minty,
"We don't want to get a chill."
And with that they all went back inside,
to eat and drink their fill.

Spike lay in his bed, but he couldn't sleep, he was too nervous about the Pony Of Christmas Yet To Come coming to visit him.

"What if in the future I have no friends like the poor little pony on the other side of Ponyville? What if no one wants to play with me? What if I'm all alone!? I don't want this last visit!" Spike said to himself.

He jumped up out of bed and ran around his castle. Making sure that all the doors and windows were locked.

"There!" he said to himself, "There's no way anybody is getting in here now!"

Spike went back to his bed and climbed in. He was so tired from all the excitement that he fell straight to sleep.

A little while later, Spike woke up feeling very cold. He pulled his bed covers up over his head, but he was still too cold.

"Mmmm!" he said to himself, "I must have left the window open!" He sat up in bed and went to stand up but as he looked down at his feet, he saw that he was standing in snow! Somehow his bed had been moved! He was outside and the snow was falling heavily all around him.

"Hello!" Spike yelled, "Is anybody there?"

Spike turned around and his bed had gone. He couldn't see anything because the snow was so thick!

He began to wander out into the snow. He was really quite scared now. He knew how easy it was to get lost in weather like this.

"Help!" Spike cried, "Please will somebody help me? I'm lost in the snow and I don't know where I am!"

Spike wondered around in the blizzard for what felt like
hours. He was so so cold and very scared. Just when he
thought all hope was lost, he heard a voice.
"Spike darling. Follow my voice. Follow my voice."
Spike looked up but he still couldn't see anybody. He
waded his way through the snow drifts towards where
the voice had come from. "That's it Spike" said the
voice, "Come this way!"
Spike began to run towards the strange voice. He ran so
hard and so fast that he did not see the castle wall in
front of him and he bumped straight into it!
"Owww!" he yelped, "That hurt my head!"
Spike looked at the castle and saw that it was his castle!
"How did that happen" he wondered, "Oh well at least
I am home now."
Spike went to his door and tried the handle, but it
wouldn't open.
"What is going on?" he asked out loud. Of course, no
one answered him.
"I know," he said "I'll try the window." Spike ran round
the castle to the window and tried to open it, but again,
the window wouldn't open. It was stuck fast.

Spike suddenly remembered. He had locked all the doors and windows to keep the Pony Of Christmas Yet To Come from visiting him.

"Oh no" Spike cried, "I'm stuck out here in the freezing snow! What will happen to me."

Just then the door opened to his castle. In the doorway stood the most beautiful pony he had ever seen. Her hair was every colour of the rainbow. It was Rainbow Dash.

"Hello Spike darling" she said.

"I am the Pony Of Christmas Yet To Come" replied Rainbow Dash, "I'm here to show you what you future Christmas' will be like." Rainbow Dash led Spike into his castle and into his dining room.

Spike walked into the room and saw himself, looking a little older, sat at his dining table all alone. He had just a candle to keep him warm, just like the pony on the other side of Ponyville. He looked so miserable, sat there all alone. No presents, no decorations, no sign of Christmas at all.

"Oh Rainbow Dash, I look just like the pony Pinkie Pie showed me!" cried Spike. "I don't want to be alone, I want to have all my friends here, celebrating with me.

"But you don't like Christmas do you Spike?" said Rainbow Dash.

"I do, I do!" cried Spike. Spike was so upset that he burst into tears. Rainbow Dash put her arm around him and gave him a big hug.

"Do you remember what Pinkie Pie said to you?" asked Rainbow Dash.

"No" sobbed Spike, "I don't remember."

"She said that the future is not set in stone. You can still change it."

"How, please tell me how" begged Spike.

"Come with me Spike" said Rainbow Dash, "let's see what the other ponies are doing."

Spike and Rainbow Dash walked out of Spike's castle. It had stopped snowing but there was no one to be seen.

"Where is everyone?" asked Spike, "It's Christmas Day, shouldn't everyone be out and about wishing each other a merry Christmas and giving each other presents?

"Well Spike," said Rainbow Dash, "No one wants to celebrate Christmas anymore."

"Why is that?" asked Spike.

"Because it was on Christmas Day that you locked yourself away in your castle and never came out to play again!" answered Rainbow Dash.

"But why would that stop people celebrating Christmas?" asked Spike.

"Spike," said Rainbow Dash looking him straight in the eye, "Christmas isn't about presents or decorations or who can eat the most roasted chestnuts. It's about being with the ones you love."

"Oh" said Spike.
"When you locked yourself in your castle all those years
ago, everyone felt so bad that they decided not to celebrate
anymore. No more parties, no more 'Merry
Christmas'. They all miss you terribly and
Christmas time reminds them all of that."
Rainbow Dash said.
"I didn't know you all cared that much,
I feel terrible now!" said Spike.
"It's not too late to change the future
Spike" said Rainbow Dash with a smile.

Pony's Ice Cream Bowl

Here are Wysteria and Scootaloo sharing a big bowl of ice cream. Unfortunately, the ice cream has no flavour. Colour in the two Ponies the way you think they should be, and then colour in the ice cream according to the flavours you think they might like.

Christmas day in Ponyville

Christmas day had arrived at last,
so all the ponies took the chance,
to all shake hands and swap their gifts,
to wish each well, and hug and kiss.

Flower gave her purse to Minty,
which, with its glitter, was very pretty.
Cupcake gave all her friends a cake,
Bumbleberry - berries to bake.

Fluttershy gave all friends the same -
a photo in a silver frame.
Then Minty gave to Daisy May,
a costume for her newest play.

Daybreak gave some chocolates to share,
Twinkle bloom - each, a teddy bear.
Sweet Breeze offered all her perfume,
that wafted through the tiny room.

Cherry Blossom, gave each a rose,
Star catcher - each, a Rudolph's nose.
Sky Wishes wrapped, each with a hug,
Fizzy gave all a hand made rug.

When all done, they went to the park,
and had some fun, until it was dark.
Then they went back to Minty's for roast,
and lifted their drinks - to toast to their host.

Spike and Rainbow Dash made there way back through the snow to Spike's castle. "So Spike," Rainbow Dash asked, "Do you understand what Christmas is all about now?" "Oh yes," said Spike, "but I'm still not sure what I should do to change my future Christmas" As Spike turned to ask Rainbow Dash what he should do next, she disappeared. Spike walked into his castle and up to his room.

"Oh dear" he thought to himself, "I have no idea what I will do now! I wish one of the ponies could have told me how to change the future."

Spike lay his head on his pillow and quickly fell asleep.

"Hurrah, Hurrah!", "Bravo Bravo!" "Encore, Encore!"

Spike woke to the sound of thunderous applause. He was sat in his chair in the theatre! He had slept through the whole Christmas play and now everyone was clapping and saying how good it was.

"Spike. Spike!" Rainbow Dash, Pinkie Pie and Star Catcher were calling to him to come up on stage. Spike rubbed his eyes and tried to wake up properly. He got up on stage and asked "What's going on?"

"What's going on?" said Star Catcher, "The play was a hit Spike!"

"Yes," chimed in Pinkie Pie, "all your hard work paid off, the show was a total success!'

"But...but...I was just with you, in the future" Spike said to Rainbow Dash.

"What Spike?" Rainbow Dash asked, "Are you feeling alright?"

"I'm not sure" said Spike.

"Spike you need to make a speech Darling" said Rainbow Dash.
"Yes, as the director of the play you have to say something" said Pinkie Pie.
"Speech, speech" yelled the crowd. Spike composed himself and moved to the front of the stage. He lifted up his hands and the audience fell silent.
"Thank you, thank you," said Spike, "I'm not sure what to say. I never really liked Christmas, it is not one of my favourite times of year. I have never liked all the rushing around and all the parties that you have to go to. When I was a younger dragon, I didn't celebrate Christmas and I never really have since. But from today that is all going to change. I have been on journey this evening and I have learnt the true meaning of Christmas."

Some of the ponies in the crowd were looking at Spike as if he had gone mad. "I have visited the Christmas' of the past, the present and the future! I have seen the joy and the sorrow that Christmas can bring. I now understand that Christmas isn't about the presents, it isn't about who has the prettiest decorations. It's about spending time with the ones you love the most, your friends and family. Everyone here is my friend and I love each and every one of you. So. I would like to invite everyone back to the castle for a big Christmas Day party! Please do all come along!"

The crowd cheered and some of the cast lifted Spike onto their shoulders. They carried Spike all the way out of the theatre and back to his castle.

Later that day, Spike's Christmas party was in full swing. All the ponies in Ponyville were there, dancing and singing, enjoying spending time with their friends.

"Spike," said Pinkie Pie, "What did you mean earlier when you said you had seen the Christmas' of the past present and future?"

"I think I must have fallen asleep in the theatre and had a dream" Spike said, "I dreamt that you, Star Catcher and Rainbow Dash all visited me in the night and taught me the true meaning of Christmas."

"That sounds like a very special dream," said Star Catcher, "was it a good dream?"

"Some of it was very happy," said Spike, "but some of it made me really quite sad."

"How?" asked Rainbow Dash joining the conversation.

"Well," Spike said, " not everyone is as lucky as we are, some people don't have any friends to celebrate with. In my dream I saw this one little pony who was all alone at Christmas and very sad."

"Who was she?" the three ponies asked?

"I don't know her name" said Spike, "but I think she lives on the other side of Ponyville."

"Are you sure?" asked Rainbow Dash, " It was only a dream and all the ponies from Ponyville are already here."

"I don't know," said Spike, "I'm not sure if it was real or not, but I think I should try and find her!"

Spike grabbed a large present from under his Christmas tree and ran out of his castle. He ran through Ponyville, over the Rainbow River Bridge and past the velvety green meadows that were covered in a thick layer of snow. He tried his hardest to remember where the poor little ponies house was in his dream, but he just couldn't. He was about to give up when he heard a tiny little cough. He turned around to see the exact house he had seen in his dream. He quietly walked over to the house and peered inside. It was just like in his dream. All alone, sat at a table with only a candle for warmth was a little pony, as he watched her the pony began to cry.

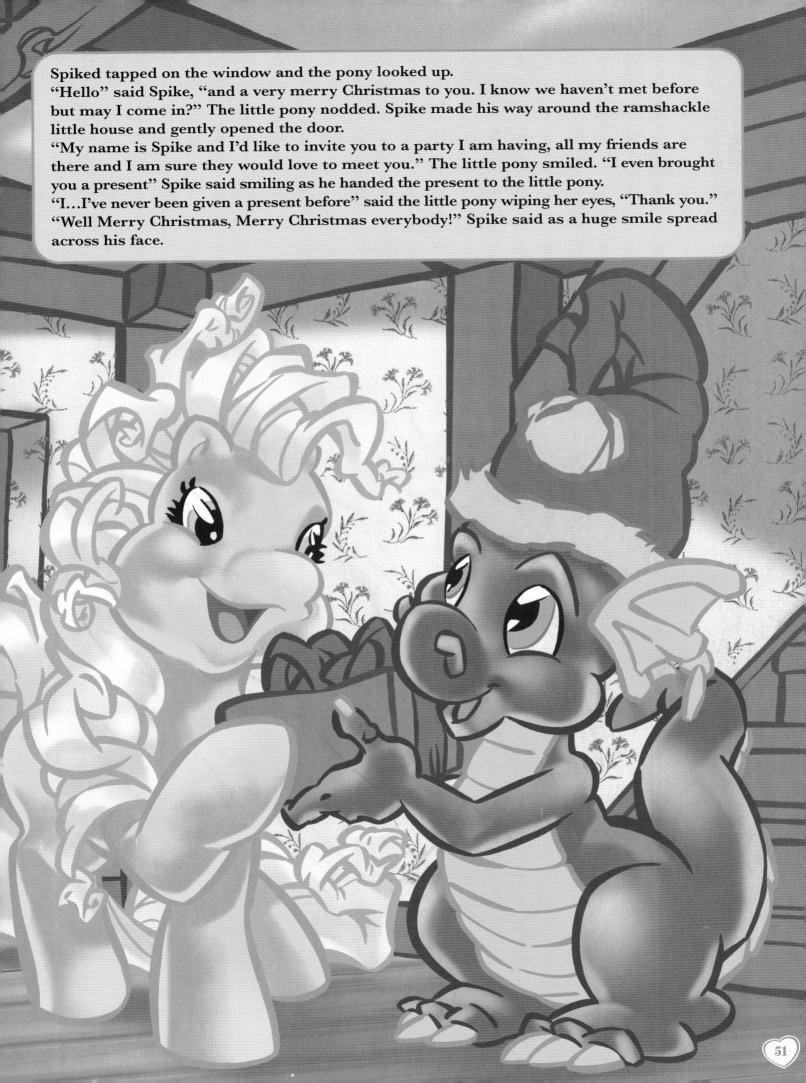

Spiked tapped on the window and the pony looked up.

"Hello" said Spike, "and a very merry Christmas to you. I know we haven't met before but may I come in?" The little pony nodded. Spike made his way around the ramshackle little house and gently opened the door.

"My name is Spike and I'd like to invite you to a party I am having, all my friends are there and I am sure they would love to meet you." The little pony smiled. "I even brought you a present" Spike said smiling as he handed the present to the little pony.

"I...I've never been given a present before" said the little pony wiping her eyes, "Thank you."

"Well Merry Christmas, Merry Christmas everybody!" Spike said as a huge smile spread across his face.

Pony Dot-to-Dot

Rarity's Copy Colour

Here are two pictures of Rarity the Unicorn - one that is coloured, and one that is not. See how closely you can copy her colours using felt-tips, coloured pencils or crayons.

55

Wysteria's Wayward Wander

Wysteria has become lost while wandering alone in the woods. Can you help her to find her friends?

Flower Garland's Colour-In

Flower Garland loves sparkly, bright and colourful things. The only thing she likes more than looking at these things, is wearing them. How do you think Flower Garland would like to look? Try to decorate her yourself, using the brightest, most colourful pencils you have.

Meet the Ponyville Ponies

Flower Garland

Flower Garland is probably one of the 'fanciest' of all the ponies. Her love of all things sparkly and bright has led her to collect — and decorate with glitter and jewels — beautiful purses, that she gives to her friends for their birthdays. She even puts special presents inside each purse.

Daybreak

Daybreak is up and out of bed bright and early every morning. The reason she gets up so early is that she never wants to miss seeing the first rays of sunlight over the fields of Ponyville. Rain or shine, she will be there every morning, watching the butterflies and listening to the morning bird song.

Star Surprise

As well as loving to watch movies with her friends, Star Surprise is also Ponyville's resident moviemaker. Whenever she gets the opportunity, she will round up her friends and ask them to act in her movies, sometimes acting alongside them, and sometimes directing the scenes. Whichever she does, her caring, kind nature makes her a very popular friend.

Tangerine Twinkle

Tangerine Twinkle is another of the ponies who loves to dance. She loves dancing so much in fact, that she can often be seen dancing along down the street. Whenever anybody asks her why she doesn't walk, she simply replies that there is no need to walk when you can dance. One year, she even won every dance contest in Ponyville!

Thistle Whistle

Thistle whistle is possibly the shyest of the Pegasus ponies and she can take a long time to make up her mind. Whenever she's having trouble deciding what she should do, she will generally whistle, which is how she gained her name. Although quiet and timid most of the time, Thistle Whistle is always quick to help a friend.

Star Catcher

Star Catcher, as well as being one of the most beautiful of all the Pegasus ponies, is also one of the most eager to help her friends and enable their dreams to come true. It was Star Catcher who made friends with Sky Wishes, and brought the Pegasus ponies and Ponyville ponies together in friendship.

Twinkle Bloom

Twinkle Bloom is a Pegasus pony that loves to dress up. Her favourite place to do this is backstage at the theatre, where there are plenty of costumes for her to try on. Twinkle Bloom has been known to forget that she is in fancy dress however, and has often been seen walking through town dressed as a cowgirl or butterfly.

Daisy May

Daisy May is an excellent flyer and regularly shows off her skills to the ponies on the ground below her. She is also very fond of performing on stage and loves to organise (and star in) talent shows in order to entertain her friends. Despite her eagerness to perform, it is not vanity which fuels her passion, but the satisfaction of seeing her friends having a good time.

Slip and Slide
BOARDGAME

5

7

4

8

1

2

9

32 31 29 28 27

33

34 36 38 39

60

Everybody likes ice-skating, but it's easy to fall over on the slippery ice if you're in a hurry. Find your self some dice and counters, and race a friend across the ice. The object of the game is to avoid the slippery patches and aim for the short cuts as you proceed along the ice. If you are able to land on a magical rainbow square, you will be able to move two more spaces forward. If you land on a slippery snowball square, you must miss a turn while you pick it up and throw it! Good luck!